# THE BIG FAT SMELLY OGRE

## GILLIAN JOHNSON

Hodder
Children's
Books

A division of Hachette Children's Books

*For Snoop – a proper little monster*

The whole thing started with a sneeze.

ACHOO!

And before you could say,

## 'COVER YOUR MOUTHS, CHILDREN!'

FOUR sneezy snufflers were sent straight to Sister Winifred's house at the edge of the school grounds.

Sister Winifred greeted them warmly and showed them around. 'There is just one small thing,' she said as they entered the bathroom.

'Is that clear?'
'BUT—!' they cried.

But there would be no buts.
Sister Winifred was
on her way, shutting
the door behind her.

They were in quarantine. Which is just
a fancy way of saying that they had to stay
away from other people until they were no
longer ill.

Who ARE these sneezing snufflers? Let me introduce them with a few comments from their teachers.

SYLVIE SPARK:

'... a dragon of a girl!'

'... such a fiery temper!'

'... she slammed the door on my fingers!'

DYLAN WHIPPLE:

'... that boy needs a bath!'

'... always running to the loo.'

'...he gave me NITS!'

**CAROLYN RUTHERFORD:**

'... has that terrible witchy giggle.'

'... so bossy!'

'... she stole the sweets I gave to the new girl ...'

**TOM DUNN:**

'... is up all night reading ...'

'... or on his computer.'

'... only wakes up in class to tell me when I'm wrong!'

It is important to know that these children were boarders at a very good school and were well-known as terrible trouble-makers.

## Also important to know...!

Sylvie, Dylan, Tom and Carolyn would never, in a million years, consider themselves FRIENDS. Which is why, when they found themselves together in the same room, they WERE NOT HAPPY.

'This is the worst day of my life,' groaned Sylvie.

'And mine,' said Dylan.

'No, MINE,' said Carolyn.

'You are ALL wrong,' said Tom. 'It is by far the worst day for ME. Stuck here with you babies!'

9

'TAKE IT BACK,' ordered Sylvie.
'NO,' said Tom.
Sylvie reached for Tom's glasses

## 'GIVE THEM BACK!'

Listening outside the door,
Sister Winifred rubbed her hands
together happily. The
headmaster was right.
They were perfect
little monsters!

Tom chased Sylvie around the sitting room and into the bathroom.

He raised his arm above his head and threw his book at Sylvie.

Sylvie ducked.

The book hit the medicine cabinet and the
forbidden door flew open.

'You idiot!' cried Sylvie. 'You're going to
be in SO much trouble!'

'It wasn't **MY** fault,' said Tom.

shrieked Carolyn gleefully.

Sylvie said nothing.
For she was watching a

# dragon

fly past.

# 'OH NO!'

cried Tom. The sound of Sister Winifred's
heels clicked towards them.

'We're in for it now!' cried Dylan.

click
click
click

But Sister Winifred didn't look cross at all!

'I don't yell,' she said sweetly, 'or give detentions.'

It sounded too good to be true.

## AND IT WAS!

'You are all going to work for me in my Monster Hospital!' she continued.

'This is crazy,' cried Dylan.

'We're not doctors,' said Sylvie.

'I have great confidence in you all,' said Sister Winifred. 'For it takes a monster to know a monster ... That makes you MORE than qualified! Now LOOK!'

For the first time, the children
looked hard at what was in the
cabinet and saw that it was not a cabinet
at all. It was a window into another world.
Perched on a hill was a castle with a moat and
a drawbridge. A flag fluttered in the breeze.

**MONSTER HOSPITAL**, it said.

'My bottom is far too big to fit through,'
said Sister Winifred. 'I'll go around the
back way while all of you climb through
the cabinet.'

So Tom, Dylan,
Carolyn and Sylvie climbed
through the cabinet and into the

## magical kingdom.

They followed Sister Winifred's voice down a long corridor ...

... through a hallway
of waiting monsters ...

... to a room where Sister Winifred stood holding up four lab coats.

NO SPELLS,
MAGIC
or TRICKS
ALLOWED

'Put these on,'
she ordered. 'And
HURRY UP!'

Because walking through the
door that very moment ...

... was the biggest, sickest ogre that the children had ever seen.

# A terrible stink

filled the room.

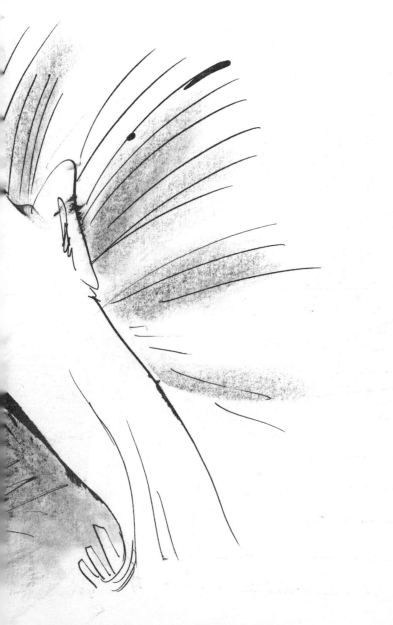

31

# 'HELP ME!
# I'm gonna DIE!'

said the ogre. Then the ogre leaned over.
"He's going to fall!" shouted Dylan.

But no.

The ogre turned around,
leaned forward and let rip an
enormous fart.
   It smelled ...

disgusting!

Tom fainted.

Carolyn giggled nervously.

Wake up, Tom!

Sylvie rolled her eyes. 'Wimps!'

... and Dylan ran to the loo.

Suddenly the click click of Sister Winifred's shoes could be heard approaching.

'Doctors! Your patient needs you!'
Sister Winifred called. 'Or perhaps I made
a mistake when I chose you for the job ...
perhaps you are not the little monsters that
I thought you were?'

She handed them a clipboard.

'Then go into the Quiet Room with this, and ask your monster questions! Find out who he is! What's wrong with him! How you can help him!'

The two girls took the clipboard ...

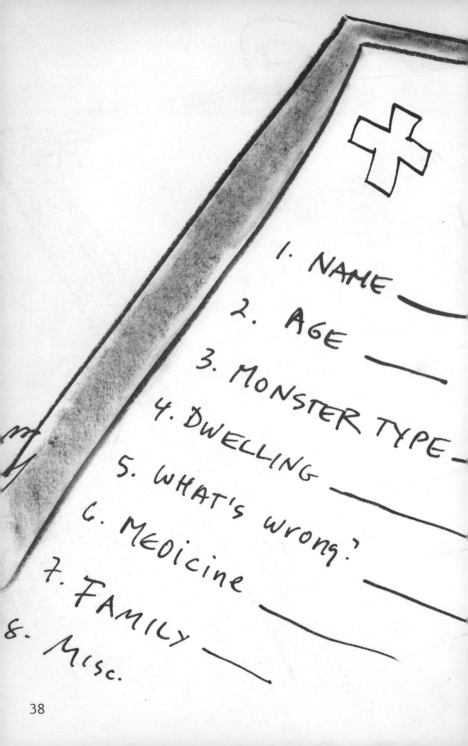

1. NAME _____

2. AGE _____

3. MONSTER TYPE _____

4. DWELLING _____

5. WHAT'S WRONG? _____

6. MEDICINE _____

7. FAMILY _____

8. MISC.

MONSTER HOSPITAL
PATIENT REPORT

... and led the ogre into the Quiet Room.

'What's your name, ogre?' asked Sylvie.

'Frank,' replied the ogre.

'How old are you?'
'About fourteen.'

'Where do you live?'
'In a cave. In the Thick Wood.'

'How did you get here?'
'Me seven-mile boots brung me,' said Frank.

'And when did this ... flatulence start?'
asked Sylvie.
'Huh?'

'She means the farts,' added Carolyn.
Frank scowled.

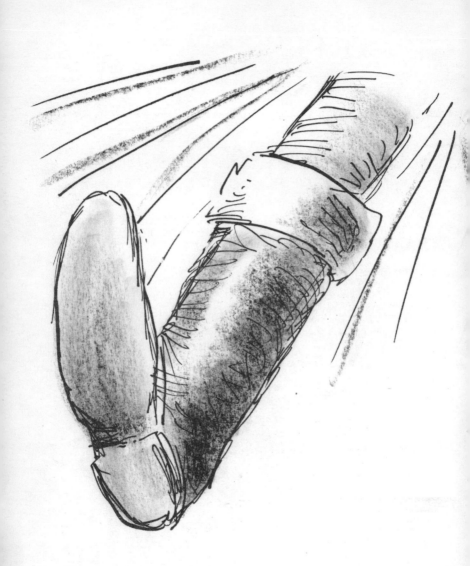

There are only so many questions a sick
ogre can answer, before he needs to ...

Fart!

The girls GASPED.

The ogre GROWLED.

'I thought you were doctors! Don't you
have some medicine for me?'

While Carolyn searched Sylvie continued
her questions.

But Frank was now in a very bad mood!

'Where is your
mother?' she asked.

DEAD!

How did
she die?

The ogre licked his bristly lips.

Sylvie tried hard not to be shocked.

'And what have YOU eaten today?'
she asked.

Frank waggled his eyebrows.

He picked his nose.

'A couple of children is all,' he said.

'They was NASTY, CRUNCHY and TOUGH!'

Then he glared down. 'As a matter of fact ... they looked JUST like you two... but not as ugly!'

Suddenly, Frank groaned.

'Pass me the medicine!' ordered Sylvie.

'Here!' said Carolyn.

TOO LATE!

It was the biggest yet.

A big booming blasting, blecky, thundering, thlopping, whoppling, blopping, whiffling, fetid, foul

FART!

The girls' eyes burned. Their throats fizzed. They fell out of the room.

'HE EATS CHILDREN!' shouted Carolyn and Sylvie.

'HIS DAD ATE HIS MOTHER! HIS LAST FART WAS ...'

'Smelly and disgusting?' asked Sister Winifred. 'Well ... he IS an ogre.' She smiled. 'Now, you girls have done an excellent job. Go and get yourselves a snack in the biscuit room. It's the boys' turn now.'

'His name is Frank!' called Carolyn, skipping off down the hall.

SNACK?

NO FAIR!

Tom and Dylan swallowed hard.

But if the girls could handle Frank,
so could they!

They went into the Quiet Room where they
found Frank looked surprisingly relaxed for a
farting-child-eating-father-ate-his-mother ogre!

'You have to come
with us,' ordered Tom.
   'To the basement.
To quarantine,' added Dylan.
   To their amazement, the ogre followed them
out into the corridor ...

... and down ...
... the crumbly stairs ...

60

... to the

DUNGEON.

Frank slumped to the floor.

'I think he's scared,' said Dylan.

'I don't know why I ever came to **MONSTER HOSPITAL**,' Frank said.

'Because you're sick with the farts,' said Dylan.

'No, that's not why.
I came because ...'

'... me seven-mile boots brung me.'

'How do they work?' asked Tom, curious.

'I dunno!' shrugged Frank. 'All ogres
have 'em. They're supposed to protect me.
Each step travels seven miles.'

His eyes filled with tears.

'Me tum! I ... I ... I ...'

His bristly lips trembled.

Frank's belly was growing.

And
# BIGGER

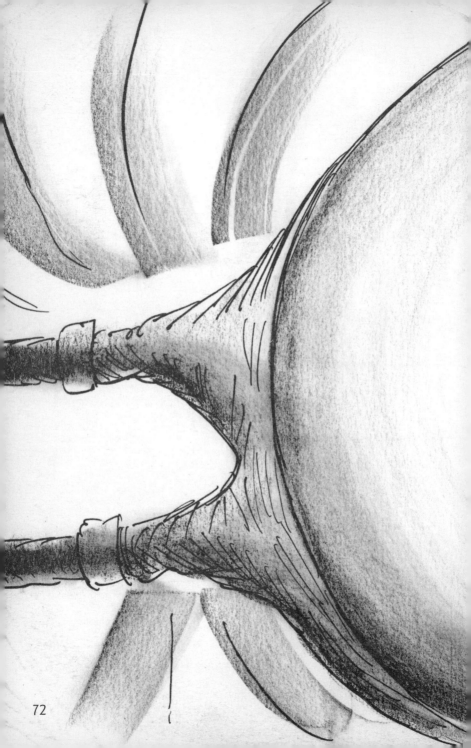

And

# BIGGER

But Dylan wouldn't leave. He was
remembering the time he had appendicitis
and his mother was far away on a work trip.
He had felt very lonely.

'I'll find your mummy, Frank,' he said
suddenly.

'**WHAT?**' gasped Tom.

Quickly, Dylan pulled off Frank's seven-mile
boots and handed one to Tom.

'He's revving up!'

Put
this on!

The boots were far too big, but it didn't matter. The boys flew out the door and up the crumbly steps and through the castle entrance ...

KA

Just in time.

Propelled by Frank's wind, the boys landed
deep in the Thick Wood.

Tom checked the GPS feature on his high-tech watch. 'We've travelled 26.4 miles already.'

But before Dylan could reply, they were off again!

The boots had a mind of their own.

# Over big hills, through deep rivers...

Across stinging beds of thorns and
**NETTLES** to a cave entrance...

Where inside they saw three ogres sitting glumly around a dead fire.

At the sight of Tom and Dylan, the
lady ogre jumped up and raised a stick.

Tom and Dylan froze.

The lady ogre took
a step closer.

Then she, too, froze ...

87

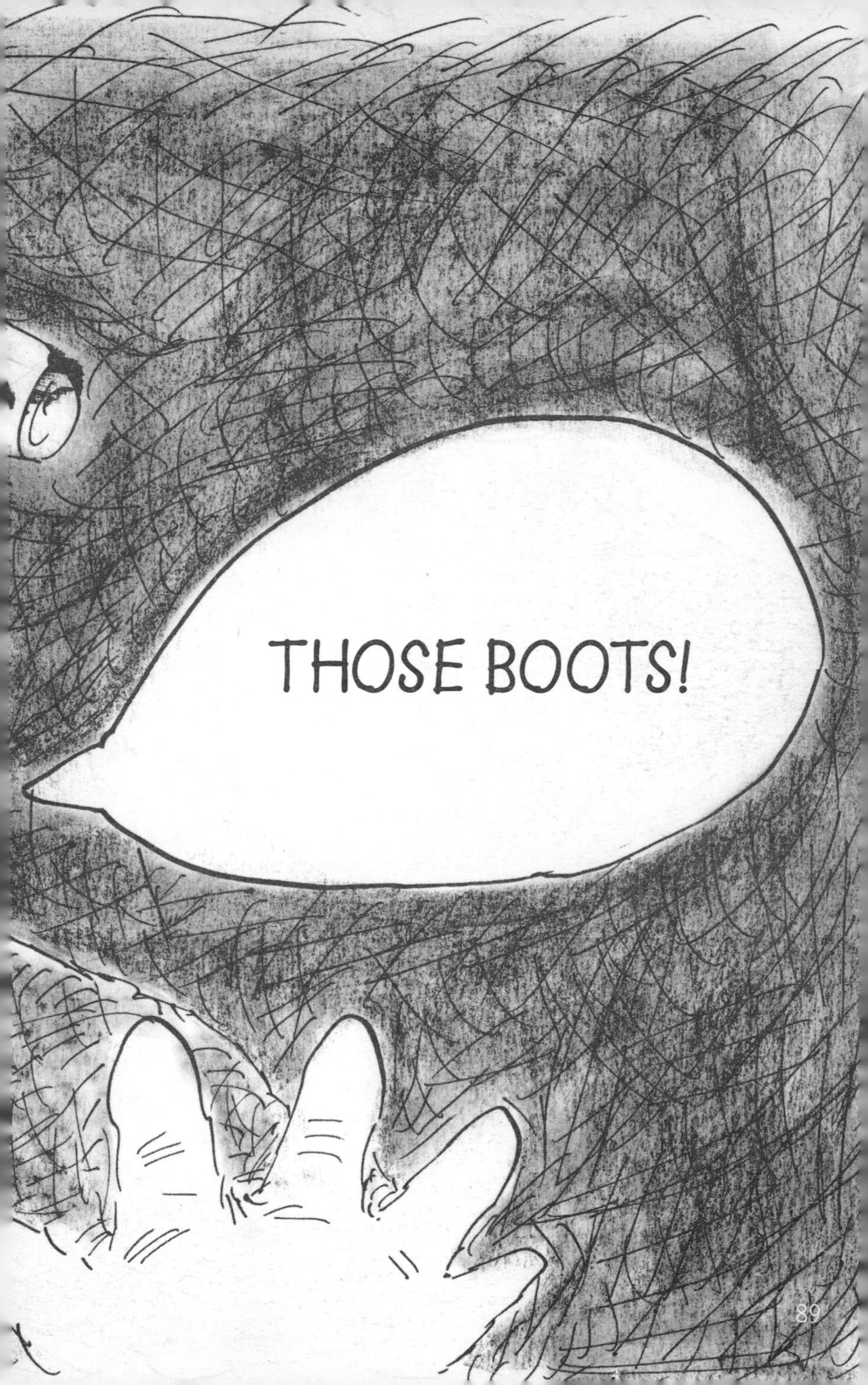
THOSE BOOTS!

Suddenly the lady ogre dropped the
stick. Her lip trembled and a tear trickled
down her cheek.

'What have you done to our big brother?'
said the little ogres.

Tom and Dylan **Shr**ank.

Would the ogres gobble them up in one bite?

'Frank has flatulence,' said Tom in a shaky voice. 'He was admitted as a patient to **MONSTER HOSPITAL**.'

'WHAT?'

'The farts!' cried Dylan. 'He's at the hospital! But he's going to get better.'

Mummy ogre picked up her stick again. 'TAKE ME TO HIM!'

So with the boys pointing the way to
**MONSTER HOSPITAL**, Mummy ogre
stepped into her own pair of seven-mile
boots and the five of them strode out
through the rain.

Meanwhile... things were not going well back at the castle.

Every time Frank farted the walls crumbled ...

And the stained-glass windows cracked.

In between explosions,
Carolyn and Sylvie held
an Emergency Meeting.
  'Let's call Sister
Winifred!' begged
Carolyn. 'She'll
know what to do.'

'No!' insisted Sylvie.
'We will do this
**OURSELVES.**'

Before Carolyn had time to burst into tears, the castle door burst open.

'Where have you BEEN?' demanded Sylvie.
'Who are THEY?' cried Carolyn.
Tom took charge. 'This,' he announced,

# 'is Frank's mother!'

'That's twins in ogre speak,' said Lydia.

The girls were stunned.
'That's impossible!' cried Sylvie.

'Frank's mother is **DEAD!**' cried Carolyn.

# 'DO I LOOK DEAD TO YOU?'

roared Lydia. 'I want to see my son. **NOW!**'

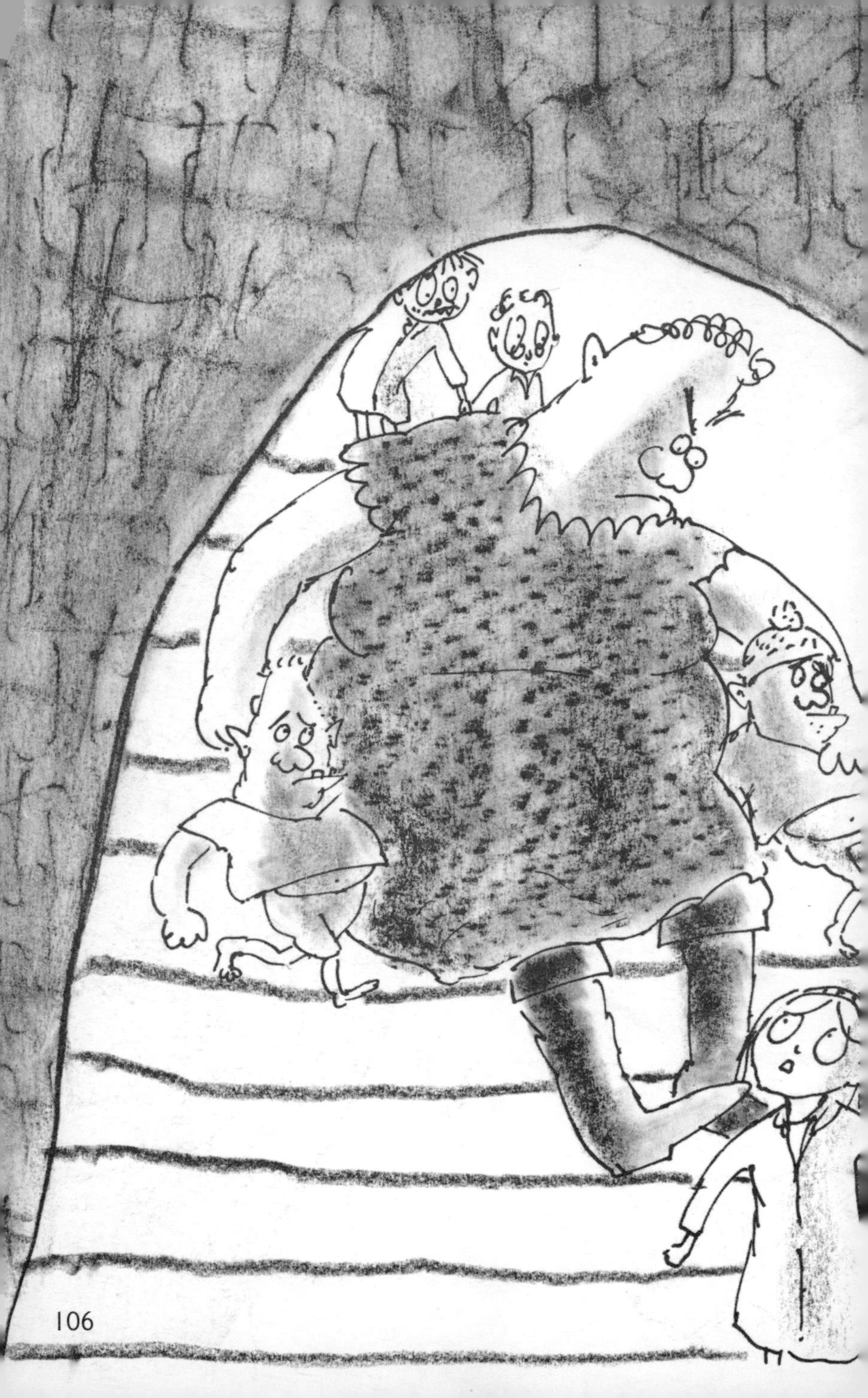

So all four doctors took Lydia
and her twigims down the
crumbly stairs ...

# To the **DUNGEON**.

'You locked him in there?' demanded Lydia.

'We had to,' said Carolyn. 'He was farting so much!'

'Farts are normal,' said Lydia.

'But they were so smelly,' said Sylvie. 'We were afraid they would destroy the castle!'

'That's my Frank,' nodded Lydia proudly. 'Smelly and strong!'

They reached the dungeon and opened the door.

**'FRANKIE!'** Lydia cried.
**'MY LITTLE TOADSTOOL!'**

'MUMMY!' blubbered Frank.

The doctors
stepped back
respectfully
as Lydia said
one embarrassing
thing after another.

Carolyn wiped her eye.
'Come on,' said Lydia to Frank. 'Let's go.
There are elves in this place.'

'Wait a minute,' warned Dylan. 'You can't just WALK OUT. Frank is ill! He's a danger to the world!'

'That's right! We put our lives at risk trying to make him better,' said Sylvie.

'Plus, he ATE two children!' said Carolyn.

The doctors nodded. For the first time ever, they all agreed.

Suddenly the twins began to chuckle.

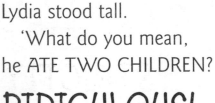

IMPOSSIBLE!

Lydia stood tall.
'What do you mean,
he ATE TWO CHILDREN?

**RIDICULOUS!**

Our ogre tribe is

# STRICTLY
# VEGETARIAN!'

For a moment, the only sound to be heard in the dungeon was the sound of mini-monsters scurrying in the shadows.

Then Sylvie spoke.

'So why did Frank tell us that he ate two kids?'

'Because he's a **TEENAGER**, you stupid
girl,' said Lydia. 'Teenagers always talk
rubbish. Especially to humans like you!'

Sylvie turned to Frank. 'Then what DID you eat for breakfast?'

'He ate beans!' said Felix.

'The whole pot!' said Francis.

'We didn't get NUTHIN!'

# 'Frank is a GREEDY GUTS!'

Over in the corner, Tom coughed.
He looked up at Lydia.
'Were they cooked?'
'Huh?'
'The beans.
Were the beans
cooked?'

Lydia turned red.
'Mummy couldn't start a fire!' blurted Felix.
'The wood was wet!' added Francis.
'The beans were raw!' they said together.

Lydia frowned.
Tom smiled.

# 'Phytohaemagglutinin poisoning!'

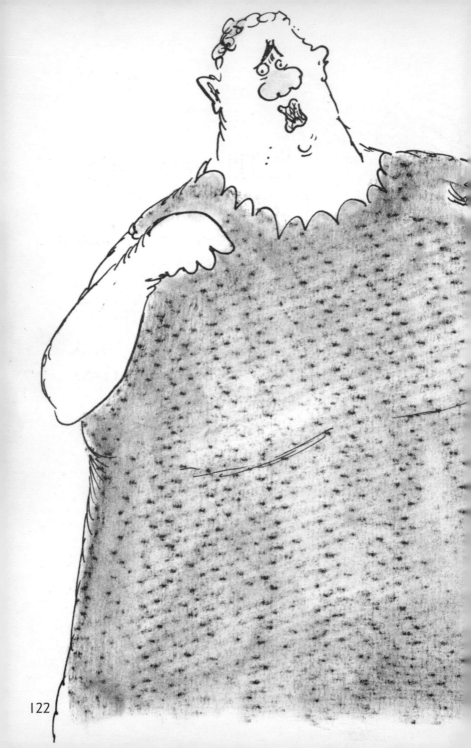

'**Poison?** Are you telling me I POISONED my own son?'

'Yes,' nodded Tom. 'Uncooked beans make monsters ... and humans ... very sick!'

'Hey,' interrupted Dylan. 'Hasn't anybody noticed? Frank hasn't farted since we've come in here!'

'No, he hasn't,' agreed Sylvie.

Lydia frowned. 'So why is his tum still so fat?' she asked. 'If it's not full of farts, what's it full of?'

'Yeah, Frank. What's in there?' shouted the twigims.

Frank looked sheepish.
'I need to go to the loo...' he muttered.
'I'll take him!' said Dylan.

Frank returned a few minutes later. He was grinning and his stomach looked a normal ogre size after his normal ogre trip to the loo.

'Let's leave now, Mum!'
'There's still something you'll need ...' said Dylan.

Tom and Dylan passed Frank his
seven-mile boots.

'Now say sorry,' said Lydia, 'for telling the doctors all those stupid lies.'

**'Sorry,'** said Frank.

click
click
click

It was Sister Winifred!

She passed around a jar of biscuits.
**'100% vegetarian!'**
she promised.

Then Frank lifted his twigim brothers, one in each arm, and carried them out of the **DUNGEON**, up the crumbly stairs, out of the castle door, and back into the Thick Wood.

Where ogres belong.

Sister Winifred turned to Tom, Dylan,
Sylvie and Carolyn. She smiled broadly.
'Now, I am sure you are all in a hurry to
return to school ...'

'Oh, you **ARE** the little monsters that I thought you were!' cried Sister Winifred.

And that was good, because coming through the door that very moment was ...

# Gillian Johnson
## answers our questions...

**Are any of the characters in *The Big Fat Smelly Ogre* based on anyone you know?**

The characters in *The Big Fat Smelly Ogre* are not based on any one person I know but are definitely combinations of people I know.

**Who's your favourite character?**

I am fond of all my characters and I am especially fond of Frank, the farting ogre.

**If you had a medicine cabinet that allowed you to go anywhere you wanted, where would it be?**

I would walk through a medicine cabinet to a place free of pain and disease.

**Where is your favourite place to write?**

My favourite place to write is the kitchen table. The problem with the kitchen table, though, is that it often has people at it who interrupt me. And there are always crumbs!

**Who are your favourite authors and illustrators, and why?**
My favourite illustrators are E.H. Shephard, Edward Ardizzone and Quentin Blake.

I have many favourite authors but if I had to choose one it would be Edward Lear for his affectionate, silly, but subtle poetry and nonsense verse. I love his inventions: words like 'scroobious' or phrases such as 'He tinkledy-binkledy-winkled a bell.'

I also love his longer poems such as *The Jumblies*: 'Their heads are green, and their hands are blue, And they went to sea in a Sieve.'

It makes me smile every time I read it.

**Tell us one thing your readers won't already know about you.**
My most recurring dream is crossing the finish line after a long running or skating race.